In honor of Johnny Depp, 100% of the roy
are being donated to Make-A-Wish®.

Make-A-Wish® creates life-changing wishes for children with critical illnesses. Make-A-Wish® is the world's largest wish-granting organization serving children in nearly 50 countries on five continents. With the help of generous donors and more than 43,000 volunteers worldwide, Make-A-Wish® has granted over 500,000 wishes to children around the globe since 1980.

For more information about Make-A-Wish®, including examples of wishes that have been granted as well as how you can donate and/or become involved as a volunteer with your local chapter, please visit www.worldwish.org.

Thank you for
Supporting
Make-A-Wish!

For my dearest Katie,

For her dear family and friends,

And for all the dear children out there,

And for all their dear family and friends, that need that little bit of extra care and understanding right now.

Please know that you are loved and that we are thinking of you all!

With all my love, my respect and my good wishes to you, always...

johnny

To my family: Given & Chosen

Illustrations and book design by Jay Howcroft

Thumper's London Adventure

Katie Vandrilla

Jay Howcroft

London was grander than Thumper had expected. He'd never been in a city and was fascinated by the new sights. This was an exciting trip for his whole family, as it was their first time outside of America.

Katie hugged Thumper firmly as they followed her mom through the crowded train station.

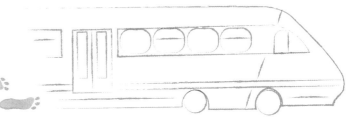

They stopped at a café. Above them was a giant clock with letters on its face. Katie's dad seemed to be planning something as he stared at the clock.

"I'll drop our bags at the hotel. You explore a bit and we'll meet under Big Ben at noon."

"These clocks don't have numbers. How will we know what time it is?" Katie asked.

"It's a different way to write numbers called Roman Numerals. 'I' is 1, 'V' is 5, and 'X' is 10. If a greater number comes before a smaller number, like 'VI,' you add them together. 'VI' is five plus one, equaling six. If the smaller number comes first, you subtract it. 'IX' is one taken away from ten, making nine."

Katie's mom was a very good teacher but Thumper was only just learning to read a regular clock.

"The short hour hand is almost on the nine, so is it close to nine right now?" asked Katie. Katie was picking up on Roman Numerals quicker than Thumper. He'd have to practice.

"Yes," said Mom. "Once the long minute hand gets to the 'XII,' the 12, it'll be the new hour. At noon, both hands need to be straight up on the twelve."

Katie's dad checked his watch.

"Do you want me to put Thumper away so you won't drop him?"

"Yes, please!"

Katie's dad strapped Thumper into the front of her backpack. What he didn't realize was that the clip didn't fully snap into place. As Katie's family separated, Thumper began to slip...

By the time Thumper knew what was happening, he was on the ground.

Oh no! Which way had Katie gone?

Thumper searched the crowd. He thought he saw her purple backpack heading towards an "Underground" sign. He tried to follow, but couldn't keep up.

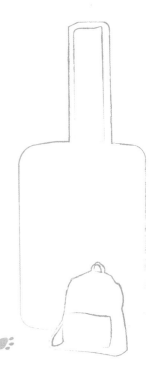

How would he find Katie in such a large city?

Big Ben!

He had to get there by noon. But where was "Big Ben"?

Katie must have boarded a train, so Thumper hopped on the first one that arrived. While the train sped from one station to the next, Thumper thought of how he would locate Big Ben. Katie's mom had read to them about London on the plane ride over.

Big Ben is a large bell inside a beige clock tower. The tower is about 100 meters tall, and the bell rings every hour.

How big is 100 meters?

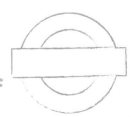

The train spoke as it pulled into another station. "Please mind the gap between the train and the platform."

Thumper got off to search for Big Ben. It was drizzling when he got outside. On the corner there was a red clock tower.

That's the wrong color. It can't be it.

The hour hand was almost on the "X" and the minute hand was pointing to the twelve.

What was "X"? ... Ten? It's already ten? I have to get moving!

A double decker bus pulled up. Thumper thought it was fun that the bus had two levels. He climbed to the top.

I'll see everything from here!

London was busy. He would have enjoyed it more if he were with Katie. Along the way, it stopped raining and the sun began to come out.

"Oxford Street. Last stop. Everyone off."

Thumper was on the busiest street he had ever seen. People were rushing in and out of stores and pushing past him.

He looked up and saw a blue and gold angel holding a clock. The hour hand was past the ten now, and the minute hand was pointing directly down.

It's half past ten and I don't see Big Ben anywhere! I have to move more quickly.

A black cab pulled up. As a passenger was loading her bags into the back seat, Thumper decided to sneak in.

When he jumped in, his paw almost landed in something sticky.

That was close!

The taxi stopped in front of a magnificent cathedral. A clock began to chime as Thumper left the cab.

"XI!" Ten plus one... It can't be eleven already!

Thumper overheard two British women.

"We have to hurry if you want to see Big Ben. Our tour of Elizabeth Tower starts soon."

They'll take me right there!

He hopped into one of their shopping bags.

"I thought you were joking. You know I'm scared of heights."

"It's only 334 steps to the top. You'll be fine."

Thumper peeked out of the bag to look around. This was the most incredible place!

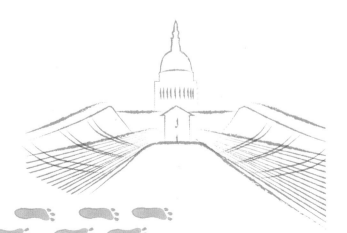

The trio boarded a boat which took them down the river. As they rounded a bend, a tall beige clock tower came into view.

That must be Big Ben!

When he got closer, he noticed both hands were almost on the twelve.

It's beautiful!

Thumper spotted Katie and her family walking by the tower.

Katie!

The women got off at the next pier and carried Thumper across a street bustling with buses, cars, and people riding bicycles. He was relieved he didn't have to dodge traffic on his own.

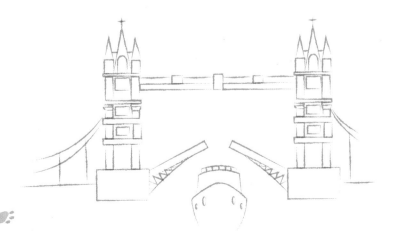

He ran up behind Katie and hopped onto her backpack. He tried holding on, but couldn't get a good grip. He landed on the pavement.

Just then, Big Ben began to chime.

"Daddy!"

Katie's dad joined them underneath the tower. "Let's take a picture," he suggested.

"I'll get Thumper." Katie put her backpack on the ground, but Thumper was nowhere to be found. "Where is he? His strap was unhooked!"

Katie's mom comforted her. "We'll retrace our steps. He couldn't have gotten far on his own."

Katie's eyes began to water. "What if we never find him?"

Her dad spotted something. "Look over there!"

"Thumper!"

Katie hugged him tighter than ever.

For the first time since they arrived in London, Thumper felt right at home.

Acknowledgements

I want to thank my parents: Kathy and David, and my brother DJ. They are there at my best and tolerate me at my worst. They've also been on every great adventure Thumper has had, constantly supporting and encouraging him to try new things.

Thank you Thumper for inspiring these stories and continuously exploring.

A huge thank you to Jay, who once again brought Thumper to life with your beautiful illustrations. Your friendship and talent are priceless blessings (and not *just* because we're donating our royalties)!

I want to acknowledge the special people in my family's life who came in and embraced our relationship with Thumper instead of running away. Thumper is a unique bunny we're happy to share. And to all humans who give their plushies life: you make the world more delightful.

A London adventure wouldn't be complete without a shout out to my friends, Jan and Carmel, who always indulge in taking me around the city when I visit. Our expeditions ('getting lost') mean the world to me. And to my wonderful fiancé, Jake: I can't wait for own London adventures.

To everyone who has assisted with or followed Thumper's story since 'Thumper's Hospital Adventure,' or is just joining us: thank you. Thanks for helping us support Make-A-Wish® and giving us an excuse for a sequel...beginning of a series???

As always, I want to acknowledge everyone at Make-A-Wish® for all that they do to make magic happen daily. My wish changed my life in countless ways (such as introducing me to London). I only hope every eligible child can have an experience as remarkable as mine.

And of course, Johnny Depp. I'm forever indebted to you. You're my inspiration to be my best self every day. Thank you.

Thumper's Scrapbook

TOWER BRIDGE

CITY OF LONDON

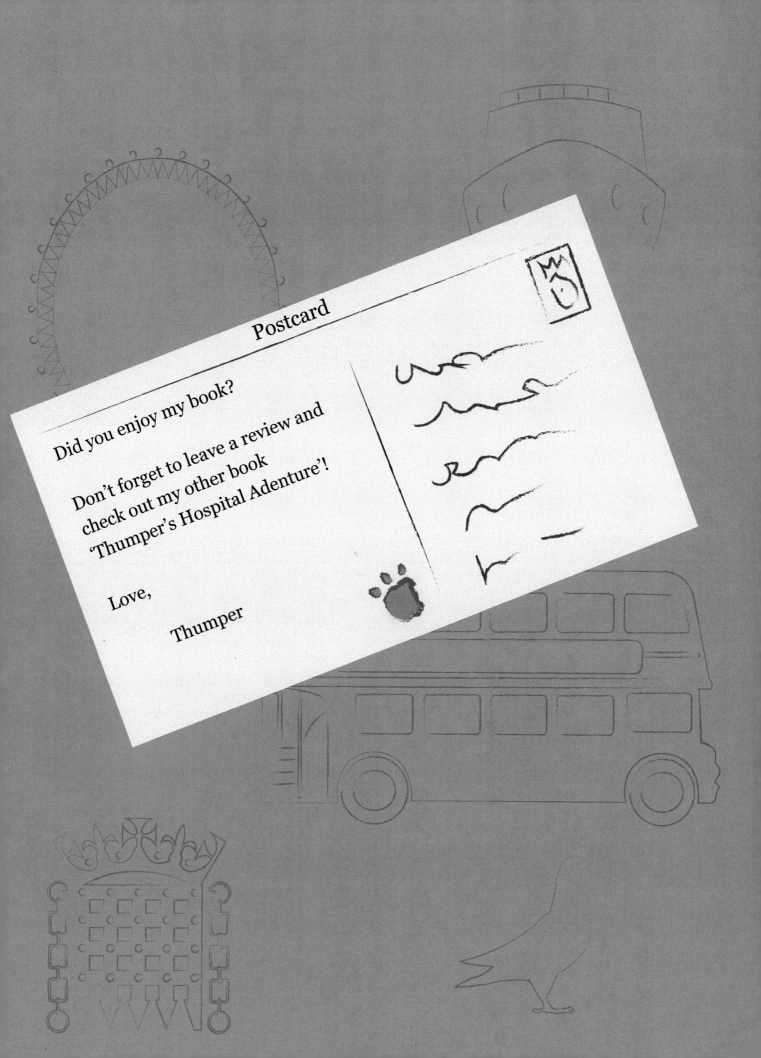

Postcard

Did you enjoy my book?

Don't forget to leave a review and
check out my other book
'Thumper's Hospital Adenture'!

Love,

Thumper

Made in the USA
Middletown, DE
23 July 2022